SPELL SISTERS:
SOPHIA THE FLAME SISTER

Amber Castle

Illustrated by Mary Hall

First published in 2012
by Simon and Schuster UK Ltd
A CBS COMPANY
This Large Print edition published by
AudioGO Ltd 2012
by arrangement with
Simon and Schuster UK Ltd

ISBN: 978 1471 306457

British Library Cataloguing in Publication Data available

Printed and bound in Great Britain by
MPG Books Group Limited

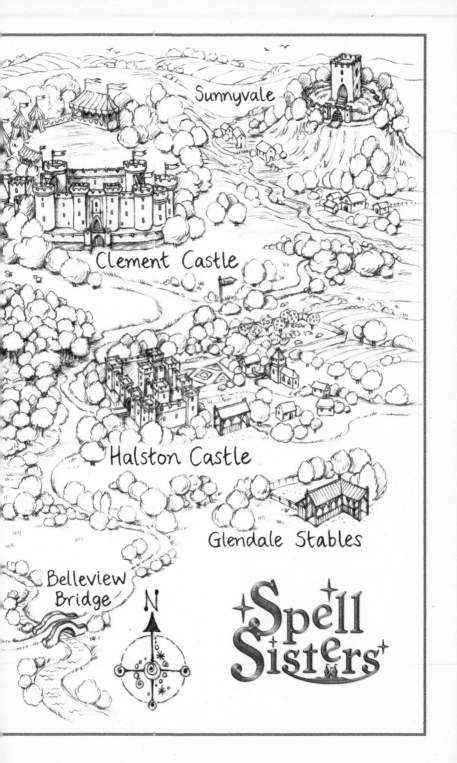

Prologue

Deep in the forest, the magical Lake glittered in the early morning sun. Tall trees stood like silent guards around the water's edge, thick branches keeping out all but the most determined of visitors. In the middle of the Lake, a purple mist swirled around. The figure watching from the bank knew just what the mist concealed. . .

'Avalon!' the woman whispered. Her dress was long and black, decorated with dark jewels that seemed to greedily draw in the light from around her. Although the early autumn air was cold, the woman wore no cloak and not a single shiver crossed her pale skin. Her cruel lips caught in a smile. 'Mine. All mine!'

Slowly, she rose into the air. She hovered for a moment and then began to drift out across the Lake. Triumph lit up her eyes as she floated across the surface but, only moments from the shore, she seemed to hit an invisible wall. With a frustrated cry, she rebounded backwards, her face creasing with rage. 'Nineve!' she growled furiously.

The shimmering waters parted and a beautiful young woman rose up through them. She was dressed in flowing blue and green robes. Her long chestnut hair almost reached down to her feet, caught back from her face by a headband of silvery pearls. A sparkling blue pendant on a silver chain hung round her neck. She met the other woman's gaze, her own eyes bright and powerful. 'You know you shall not pass, Morgana!' Her clear voice rang out across the water. 'My spell prevents it.'

'Not for much longer, Nineve!' Morgana hissed, pointing her finger at the Lady of the Lake. 'It has been eleven moons since you cast your spell and it is weakening. The lunar eclipse approaches, then your magic will fade completely and my sisters be imprisoned forever!' Morgana's voice rose. 'And finally Avalon shall be mine!' Clapping her hands, she swirled around and vanished.

Nineve, the Lady of the Lake, stared at where Morgana had been, a troubled look on her beautiful face. Morgana was right. The spell would not last much longer. If the sisters of Avalon were not freed from Morgana's evil enchantments by the time the next lunar eclipse began, the magical island would come under Morgana's control and its special powers lost to the world forever.

'That cannot be allowed to happen.' Nineve's fingers reached for the blue pendant at her throat, the aqua stone changing in colour like the deepest ocean reflecting changes in the light. Nineve thought for a moment and then came to a decision. It was her last hope. Only a mortal could save Avalon now—it was written in the stars. The Lady of the Lake took a deep breath, and recited the ancient prophecy:

*'When darkness threatens the world
    we know,
And Avalon's bright lights cease to
    glow,
Seek out a girl who is true and brave,*

She will be the one who shall our kingdom save.'

Nineve unclasped the necklace and then, moving to the edge of the water, she knelt down beside a smooth black rock. Holding the chain in her left hand, she placed the pendant on the rock and passed her right hand in a circle over the top of it.

There was a silver flash and the pendant slowly sank into the surface of the stone. Nineve watched intently. As it disappeared from view, she waved her hand over it again and the movement stopped. The blue pendant was now hidden in the stone, but the chain still remained on the surface.

'Lie here until the one who can save Avalon releases you,' murmured Nineve. 'She will be our last chance.' She stood up and stared down at the silver chain. 'May she come soon.'

Turning, Nineve drifted slowly out across the water until she was lost in the swirling purple mist . . .

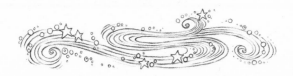

The Last Laugh!

'Straighten your back, Guinevere and let me see you curtsey again.'

'Yes, Aunt Matilda.' Gwen took a deep breath. She really didn't like it when her Aunt used her full name. Her green eyes flicked to the small window in her aunt's bedchamber. She could see sunlight outside and hear the voices of the pages as they practised riding on the ponies from the castle stables. She wished she could be out there with them.

Casting her eyes down, she curtseyed again for her Aunt Matilda.

'Better!' her elegant aunt said approvingly. 'But, chin down more and gaze to the floor, dear.'

Gwen held the pose as her aunt inspected her curtsey. She hated the fact that as a girl she was supposed to spend her time learning boring things like how to curtsey gracefully. She had to attend to her aunt and the other women who lived in the castle, look after their clothes, comb and dress their hair and generally learn how she must behave when she got older. She knew her parents had her best interests at heart when they sent her to live with Aunt Matilda and Uncle Richard at Halston Castle, but she still couldn't get used to the duties expected of her.

The voices of her uncle's pages came floating up to her from the courtyard.

'Ride faster, Arthur!'

'Here! Use this sword!'

'Try and hit it, Will!'

Gwen yearned to be down there with them. The boys always got to do exciting things! She wondered which pony they were riding. Luckily, girls were allowed to learn how to ride and she often went to the stables to see the horses and ponies. Gwen had even tried riding bareback like the boys sometimes did. She'd tried it when she'd been in the forest on her own a few days ago with one of the ponies. She'd loved it, but knew no one must ever find out or she'd be in real trouble—it simply wasn't lady-like behaviour. She hadn't even told her cousin, and best friend, Flora. Gwen smiled to herself as she imagined how alarmed well-behaved Flora would be if she knew!

'Guinevere, it's not becoming of a young lady to grin in that way!'

Her aunt's sharp voice jolted her back to the present. Gwen hastily adjusted her expression. If she wanted to be allowed to leave her aunt's bedchamber, she knew she had to try her hardest to please.

To her relief, her aunt finally nodded approvingly. 'Well done, my dear. Now, help me fix my hair and then you can go outside.'

Aunt Matilda sat down at her dressing table, adjusting the brooch that fastened her long red cloak to her shoulders. Even though the sun was shining outside and there were rugs on the floor and thick tapestries on the walls, the rooms inside the castle were always cold.

Gwen plaited her aunt's long fair hair and coiled it into a bun at the nape of her neck. Gwen's own deep red hair tumbled loose about her shoulders. Flora liked to wear her  blonde hair in two long braids—she often wound brightly-coloured cord and ribbon around them to match the colour of her dresses, but Gwen could never be bothered with things like that.

When I'm grown up I'll always wear my hair down, she thought as she finished carefully pinning up her aunt's hair. *I'm not going to fuss about like this!*

'May I go now, Aunt Matilda?' she asked as politely as she could.

'You may,' her aunt replied, inspecting her bun in the mirror.

Gwen's heart leaped and she ran to the door. 'No playing with the pages though!' Aunt Matilda called after her. 'Find Flora—walk and talk together, go and see how the winter roses are growing in the garden . . .'

Gwen heard her aunt's voice trailing after her as she raced down the spiral stone stairs. She stopped briefly in the chamber she shared with Flora to grab her thick wool cloak, outdoor boots and her leather bag. A few minutes later she was bursting through the heavy wooden door that led to the courtyard. Fresh air hit her face. She stopped and breathed it in happily, her eyes scanning the grassy yard inside the castle walls. It was so good to be outside!

The six pages who lived at the castle were in the centre of the courtyard. Noblemen's sons left their homes when they were seven to go and live in other noble households and begin the long training from page to squire to knight. The boys were standing around Basil, a round-bellied dappled pony. Beside him was a straw dummy the boys had made out of a sack that they were using to practise their sword fighting. Straw was hanging out of its ripped body, trailing across the grass. Tall, blond Arthur, who was twelve, had his arm over the pony's neck and was stroking him.

'You were brilliant, Arthur!' said one of the younger boys admiringly.

Tom, the smallest, leaped forward, stabbing the dummy with a flourish and a yell. 'I'm going to be able to use a sword like you when I'm older,' he declared.

Will, who was the eldest of the pages at fourteen, looked a bit jealous and grabbed Arthur round the neck in a sudden headlock. 'Pity you're not so good at wrestling, Arthur!' he said as he tried to flip him to the ground.

For a moment, Gwen thought he was going to succeed, but then Arthur grabbed Will's knees and pulled. The older boy's legs shot out from under him and he fell with a heavy grunt to the ground. Arthur straightened up and grinned. 'Pity you're even worse than *me*, Will!'

Gwen smiled. She really liked Arthur. Although she was a year younger than him, they had arrived at her uncle's house at about the same time and had always got along well. If they bumped into each other down in the stables and Arthur wasn't with the other pages, he would always stop to talk to her.

Will got to his feet, looking cross. Being the eldest, he didn't like being beaten by any of the others. 'Come on,' he scowled. 'Let's put Basil away and go to the forest to practise with our bows and arrows.'

Forgetting her aunt's strict instructions about not playing with the boys, Gwen went forward eagerly. 'Can I come?' She loved archery and was very good at it.

'You?' Will looked her up and down, with a faint sneer. 'But you're a girl!'

'So? I can shoot!' Gwen protested. 'You know I can, Will!'

Will snorted. 'Yes. Like a girl.' He pretended to shoot an arrow and then put on a high voice, miming looking shocked. 'Oh no, my arrow went all the way up into that big tall tree. What am I to do?'

Gwen put her hands on her hips and gave him a withering look. 'I only shot an arrow into a tree once and that was when I first started. And you know I never speak like that.'

'Go and fix your aunty's clothes or

brush her hair. We don't want a girl with us.' Will took Basil's reins and sauntered away.

'Yeah, girls can't shoot,' said one of the younger boys, joining Will.

The other pages sniggered and headed after them. Only Arthur paused and seemed about to say something.

Will realised he wasn't with them and looked round. 'Arthur! What are you doing? Come on!'

Arthur gave Gwen a sympathetic look and headed after the boys. Gwen's scowl deepened. So they didn't think she could shoot? Well, she'd show them!

She marched inside and went straight up to her bedchamber and picked up her bow. It was reddish-brown and light but strong. Soft leather wrapped around the handle. Gwen wore it slung across her body  on a strap with her quiver—a leather pouch filled with her arrows.

Gwen headed back outside and was pleased when she saw Flora walking into the courtyard, humming softly to herself and carrying a flat wicker basket full of freshly picked flowers. Flora was small with a very pretty round face and big blue eyes. Today, her two blonde braids were trimmed with fine golden cord that matched her yellow and gold dress.

Seeing Gwen, she smiled and ran over. 'Gwen! I've just been picking some flowers to make our bedchamber look prettier.'

Her basket overflowed with red blossoms, but as she reached Gwen she somehow managed to catch the bottom of her dress on her slipper and tripped over, spilling flowers everywhere.

'Bother!' she cried, standing up swiftly and brushing her skirts vigorously. 'This is a new dress!'

Gwen rushed over to help her friend gather the flowers back up, smiling gently. Although Flora always did her best to be lady-like, her clumsiness often got the better of her!

As they finished picking up the
flowers, Flora noticed Gwen's bow
and arrow. 'Are you going to do some
archery practice?'

'Not really,' Gwen said innocently,
knowing her cousin would worry. 'Well
. . . I just thought I might go for a walk
in the forest and perhaps do a bit of
practice there.'

Flora followed Gwen's gaze and saw
the boys. They had put Basil away and
were now heading out of the castle and
down the hill towards the nearby trees.
'Oh, no, you're not thinking of going
after the boys, are you? You know they
won't let you join in with them.' She

17

regarded Gwen for a moment and then sighed. 'I'm coming with you. I know what you're like—you'll do something wild if you're on your own.'

'But I'm only going for a walk!' Gwen protested.

Flora raised her eyebrows. 'And let me guess. It's a walk that might just happen to take you near to where the boys are going?'

'Maybe,' admitted Gwen.

Flora dumped her basket on the ground. 'In that case I'm definitely coming too!'

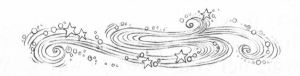

2

An Unexpected Surprise

Gwen and Flora headed out of the castle grounds chatting about what they had been doing that day and about how annoying the boys could be. As they reached the edge of the forest, Gwen felt a thrill of delight run through her. She loved the rustle of the leaves, the cracking of twigs under her boots, the way the tree branches reached out like crooked arms, and the mysterious shadows they cast. In the forest it always felt like something exciting could happen at any moment! Gwen's favourite place of all was the beautiful glittering Lake right in the centre. A mysterious island called Avalon rose up in the middle of the water, but a purple mist always swirled around it, hiding it, so Gwen had never seen the island properly. She would sit for ages staring out across the glimmering glass-like water though, simply imagining it.

Now, however, Gwen wasn't thinking about the Lake or the island. She wanted to find the boys! While Flora held up the hem of her long dress and picked her way carefully over the tree roots, Gwen marched on, her dress getting more and more damp, picking up leaves and twigs.

'Look at your skirt, Gwen!' exclaimed Flora.

'So?' Gwen swung round, arms wide for a moment, enjoying the feeling of freedom. Out here in the forest she was away from the eyes of the grown-ups in the castle. Here she could do anything! She took a deep breath of the autumnal air and felt happiness bubble through her. She stopped twirling and listened for a moment. She could hear the pages' voices in a nearby clearing.

'This way!' she urged Flora, darting off the main path and through the trees.

'But look at the brambles and the nettles and . . . oh!' Flora exclaimed in dismay as she stepped in a muddy puddle.

'Shh!' Gwen said, waving her hand at her cousin. They were getting closer now and they needed to be quiet or the boys would hear. She wanted to sneak up on them . . .

Slipping her bow off her shoulder, she clasped it lightly.

'Oh no! I've just trodden on a slug and—' Flora broke off as she saw Gwen raising her bow. 'Gwen! What are you doing?'

'Shh!' Gwen hissed again. Moving like a shadow, she slipped up to the final line of trees before the clearing.

Yes! There were the boys! The six pages were all standing on one side of the clearing. On the opposite side they had drawn a round target on a big oak tree. They were taking it in turns to try and hit it, but all their arrows were falling short or getting stuck in the tree's branches.

'So it's only girls who get arrows stuck in trees, is it?' Gwen muttered. 'Well, watch this!'

She slipped an arrow from the quiver on her back. Holding the bow almost horizontally, she rested the arrow against it, eased the notch on to the bow-string and felt it clip in. Her eyes focused carefully on the target. She raised the bow, pulling back the string with her right hand and anchoring it carefully against her cheek. Staring down the arrow to

22

the target on the tree, she breathed out . . . and released.

The arrow sliced through the sun-dappled air of the clearing. Gwen caught her breath. Was it going to hit the target?

The boys all yelled in surprise as they saw it.

Thunk! The arrow struck home, sinking deep into the wood, dead centre in the middle of the target. Gwen's face broke into a broad grin. She stepped out of the trees and stood there, hands on her hips, her green eyes flashing. 'So girls can't shoot?'

She saw the boys' astonished faces. Tossing her hair back, she went over to the tree, pulling her arrow out of the bark. She turned back with it in her hand. 'If any of you boys ever want any lessons in archery, just let me know!' Then, whistling airily, she strolled back to the trees where Flora was watching with her hand over her mouth, holding back her giggles.

'Oh, Gwen! That was wonderful!'

Hearing the pages' voices rising up behind them, Gwen giggled too.

23

'Come on!' she said to Flora. 'Let's go exploring!'

The two girls headed deeper into the forest. Flora looked around nervously. 'I don't really like going this deep into the trees,' she said after a while. 'I always think there might be things watching me from the shadows.'

Gwen pretended to hide behind a tree and jumped out at her. 'What—you mean like monsters?' she grinned.

Flora pushed her playfully. 'No, but you know what people say. We've both heard the tales.' She shivered. 'The storytellers always say that the forest is a place where magical things happen. There could be dragons or enchanters or strange spirits! Maybe . . . maybe we should go home.'

'But I want to go on to the Lake,' Gwen argued.

'Do we really have to?'

'Yes!' Gwen insisted, linking arms with Flora. 'Look, I come into the forest lots, and nothing has ever happened to me.'

Flora let Gwen lead her further into

the trees. 'I just wish it wasn't so quiet,' she said, her blue eyes darting around. 'Doesn't it feel strange to you, Gwen?'

Gwen paused for a moment. In her eagerness to get to the Lake, she hadn't noticed it, but now she had to admit that Flora was right. It was getting quieter and quieter as they headed closer to the Lake. There were no birds singing, no faint cracking of twigs as an animal passed by, and the trees' leaves were not golden and red here—they were brown and dull. A shiver ran across Gwen's skin.

'Let's go back,' said Flora, stopping suddenly. 'I don't like this.'

'No!' Gwen didn't know why, but she was suddenly filled with an urge to get to the Lake. It wasn't far away. Pulling away from Flora, she broke into a run, feeling like the Lake was somehow calling to her through the trees. She couldn't turn back now!

'Wait, Gwen!'

Gwen ignored her cousin. She jumped over gnarled roots, scrambled past thick bushes and finally pushed her way out between the trunks of the trees that surrounded the Lake. Her heart was pounding, but to her relief the Lake looked just as it usually did. The glittering water shone and a feeling of peace and quiet hung in the air.

Gwen let out a breath. For one dreadful moment she had thought that she was going to see something different—that somehow the Lake would have changed in some horrible way.

Flora appeared through the trees, a twig caught in her neat hair, a smudge on her cheek.

'It's just like it always is . . .' Gwen's voice trailed off as she spoke. No matter what she'd felt before, she was here now and she was happy to just enjoy the Lake.

Kicking off her boots, she reached under her dress and wriggled out of her woollen tights. Then, with her bare feet sinking into the short cold grass, she ran down the bank to the edge of the Lake. Holding up her skirt, she gasped as the icy water covered her toes.

Flora followed her more cautiously,

edging down the bank and going over to sit on a cluster of rocks at the side of the Lake. But, just as she was about to settle herself down, Flora let out a surprised cry. 'There's something here, Gwen, look! A silver chain!'

Gwen glanced back briefly and saw Flora crouching beside one of the rocks. 'It's probably just some lady's necklace that a magpie stole and dropped,' Gwen called over her shoulder, taking a step deeper into the water.

'It doesn't look like it's been dropped,' said Flora. 'It looks as if it's caught in the rock.'

Gwen shrugged. The Lake was so clear she could see straight down to the pebbles on the bottom. She moved her toes, making the water swirl.

'Come and see, Gwen!' Flora insisted. 'It's really strange.'

With a sigh, Gwen went over. Flora was pulling at the chain but it wouldn't budge. The rock's surface was as smooth as a mirror, and the silver chain seemed to be almost growing out of the centre of it. Gwen felt a flicker of

surprise. She'd expected there to be a crack or something that the chain was caught in, but there wasn't. Flora was right—it looked like part of the chain was actually inside the rock.

'It's stuck fast!' said Flora, giving it another tug.

'Here, let me have a go!' Gwen took the chain. As her fingers closed around the metal she could have sworn she felt a strange tingle run through her hands and up her arms. She gave a pull. With a faint clink and clatter, the chain slid easily out of the rock, sending Gwen staggering back with a surprised cry.

For a moment, Gwen stood in the water, staring at the necklace in her hands. A large blue pendant dangled from it.

'How did you do that?' Flora exclaimed. 'I pulled as hard as I could and it wouldn't move.'

Gwen was just as astonished. She stared down at the necklace. 'I . . . I don't know.' The large blue pendant seemed to glow and shine. She'd never seen anything like it. Holding it up, Gwen stared at it, her eyes wide with wonder. As she watched, the pendant suddenly seemed to twist and turn as if it had a life of its own.

Gwen jumped and dropped the necklace—but instead of it falling to the ground, it floated up into the air as if carried by invisible hands.

Flora shrieked.

Gwen's mouth fell open. For once, she was lost for words.

The pendant twirled around in the air, coming closer and closer to Gwen. It dangled in front of her face and suddenly she was filled with the urge to touch it. She reached out.

'No, Gwen, don't!' gasped Flora.

But it was too late. As Gwen's trembling fingers touched the glowing stone, there was a bright silver flash. Gwen blinked, and then heard a faint click like a clasp shutting. She felt a heaviness around her neck, and as she looked down a startled exclamation burst from her lips. The beautiful necklace had fastened itself around her neck!

Magic! Her thoughts whirled. *It's magic!*

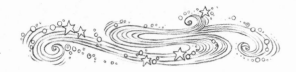

The Lady of the Lake

Gwen's fingers closed around the pendant. She couldn't explain it, but it somehow felt like it had been waiting for her—that it *belonged* to her.

'What's happening?' breathed Flora, her eyes wide.

A bright light seemed to shine out over a spot in the Lake. 'Look!' Gwen exclaimed.

They both stared as the light grew brighter and brighter, and then the waters parted. To their amazement, a beautiful young woman rose up to the surface.

Gwen stared. What was happening? Was this woman a water nymph—a spirit of the water? Or maybe she was a goddess or a sorceress? As Flora had said, Gwen *had* heard the storytellers who came to the castle telling tales of magical beings who lived throughout the land. Could it really be true?

'I . . . I don't like this!' Flora stammered, backing away.

Gwen's heart was banging against her ribs, but she was rooted to the spot. She bravely faced the woman and called out: 'Who are you?'

'My name is Nineve.' The woman's voice was low and musical. Her long chestnut-brown hair swept all the way down to her feet, held back from her face by a sparkling pearl headband. Her dress shimmered with different shades of green and blue all the way down to her bare feet. As the girls watched, she began to float across the surface of the water towards them.

Run! a small panicked part of Gwen's brain yelled—but another

34

feeling deep down inside held her still. Nineve was so beautiful and had such sparkling eyes. She gave off a feeling of peace and serenity. A thought beat through Gwen—*There's nothing to be scared of.*

Nineve stopped in front of her. 'Guinevere.' She smiled.

Gwen felt a moment's shock. 'How . . . how do you know my name?'

'I am the Lady of the Lake,' Nineve answered softly. 'And I know many things.' Her eyes fell to the pendant around Gwen's neck. 'The pendant has chosen you, Guinevere. Avalon is in danger. Only a mortal girl can save it and *you* are that girl.'

If it hadn't been for the icy water still lapping at her toes, Gwen would have been sure she was in a dream. 'Avalon? You mean the island in the Lake?'

Nineve nodded.

Flora, who had been silent with shock until this point, finally spoke. 'But why?' she asked, her voice still shaking a little. 'Why does Avalon need saving?'

'Come. I will show you.' Nineve started to float across the Lake towards the island, beckoning for them to follow.

Gwen went a few paces and then stopped. 'Wait! The water's too deep. How can we come with you, Nineve?'

A smile caught at Nineve's mouth. 'By magic,' she said softly. She clapped her hands. Instantly, a fine white mist rose from the Lake, swirling around both Gwen and Flora, spiralling up from their toes to their heads. Gwen gasped as she felt herself being lifted into the air. The mist was everywhere and for a moment all she could see was a cloud of sparkling white. Suddenly, she had the sensation that she was floating over the water, and as the mist started to clear, spiralling back down to her feet, Gwen realised that she had been right. She really was floating across the Lake's surface—Flora too! Gwen tried moving her feet and found she could move easily. She ran across the water towards where Nineve was waiting at the edge of the purple mist that still surrounded the island.

Gwen stopped beside the Lady of the Lake, her eyes shining. All her life she had wanted a real adventure, and now she was finally having one! Nineve waited for Flora to reach them too, and then she looked at the two girls steadily. 'Are you ready to see Avalon?'

Flora and Gwen looked at each other. 'Oh yes!' breathed Gwen, and Flora nodded, though she looked a little nervous. Nineve smiled, but Gwen thought she saw a sadness in her dark eyes.

Lifting her hands into the air, Nineve began to murmur a string of strange-sounding words and the purple mist parted, forming a path that led to the secret island. Nineve walked down it. Flora grabbed Gwen's hand and then they both followed. Coming out of the mist, they stepped from the water on to the solid rock of the island and looked around.

Gwen felt a shock run all the way through her. She'd always pictured Avalon as a beautiful place. The tales she had heard of it had told of a rich green island, covered with grass and apple trees and filled with the sound of birdsong. But this . . . it looked nothing like the place she'd been imagining. All she could see were grey craggy rocks, sparse clumps of grass, dried-up streams and dying, twisted trees. On a sloping hillside reached by stone steps was a large house. It too was crumbling and decaying, and its dark windows looked like empty, blank eyes. At the bottom of the stone steps was a small tree. It appeared to be the only tree on the island that still had a few green leaves. A single red apple was growing in its branches.

'Oh,' said Gwen. 'I never thought . . .' Her voice trailed off. 'I . . . I always imagined Avalon to be beautiful.'

The sadness in Nineve's eyes deepened. 'It was, Guinevere. Not long ago, it was one of the most beautiful and magical places in this realm. Nine Spell Sisters, all sorceresses, lived here. Each had their own powers and most of them used their goodness to keep Avalon's magic strong. For Avalon is very important to the world; in years to come, the kingdom will need its magic.'

Gwen and Flora looked at one another with concern. 'What do you mean, the kingdom needs Avalon?'

Gwen asked, her forehead wrinkled with concern.

'My powers allow me to see many things—past, present and future,' Nineve answered. 'I know this magical island has a vital role to play in the battle between good and evil that is to come. Even now, the loss of its magic is slowly draining the colour and life from the kingdom around us. The longer the sisters are away, the worse it will get. I cannot tell you more but, believe me, if Avalon's magic is lost then great trouble will come to all.'

Nineve paused and then gave them a small smile. 'Now watch—this is what the island should look like.'

Nineve raised her hands. For a moment the whole island seem to shimmer, and then, suddenly, it looked completely different. The grass was green and lush, the trees' branches were heavy with red and green apples, clouds of multi-coloured butterflies flitted through the air and birds sang. The house was glowing with light from inside and music echoed out through the open windows.

'It's wonderful!' Gwen gasped, looking around in awe and walking up the hillside towards the house. Nineve and Flora followed her.

'This is how Avalon used to look. It is very different from what it has become.' Nineve lowered her hands and the vision faded. Once again the island was grey and dying, a chill creeping through the air. The only splash of colour was the red of the single apple on the tree.

'But what's happened?' Gwen demanded. She hated seeing the difference between the vision and the reality. 'What happened to the Spell Sisters who lived here?'

For a moment, ice seemed to snap through Nineve's musical voice. 'Morgana Le Fay.'

'Who?' Flora asked in confusion.

'I will explain, but I'm afraid I must be quick,' Nineve answered, her face starting to look worried. 'I cannot be out of the Lake for long or my magic will weaken.' Gwen and Flora nodded, and Nineve continued. 'Almost twelve moons ago, the eldest of the nine sisters of Avalon, Morgana, tricked her younger siblings into leaving the island. She used her magic to imprison them in eight hidden locations around the kingdom, and stole their powers.'

'But why did she do that?' asked Gwen.

Nineve sighed. 'Morgana wants Avalon for herself. Now that she has the powers of all the Spell Sisters, the island will become hers and hers alone as soon as she steps foot on it. Avalon's magic, and all the sisters' abilities, will be under her control. So far, I have managed to stop her returning to the island by casting a spell that prevents her from crossing the Lake. However, it will only last until the next lunar eclipse and then Morgana will be able to take control of Avalon.'

'What will happen?' Flora said worriedly.

Nineve rubbed a hand across her forehead. 'If that happens, this once beautiful place will continue to rot and die. Morgana is evil, and the island needs the goodness of the other eight sisters in order for its own powerful magic to flourish.'

'Then we have to save it!' Gwen declared. 'What can we do to help?'

'It is up to you now,' Nineve said, her eyes fixed on Gwen's. 'The stars predict that a mortal girl will hold the balance of power in her hands. You are that girl because you were the one the pendant chose.'

'What will Gwen have to do?' asked

Flora anxiously.

'Find and free all eight Spell Sisters before the next lunar eclipse and return them to Avalon. Then good shall triumph over evil.'

Flora looked shocked. 'But how can Gwen possibly do that? If your magic can stop Morgana crossing the Lake, can't you use it to free her sisters too?'

Nineve shook her head. 'I'm afraid my magic only works while I'm in contact with the water that surrounds Avalon. Gwen will need to search the land and find each of the sisters before they can be freed.'

'But—' Flora began.

'I can do it, Flora!' Gwen exclaimed, interrupting her cousin. Courage rushed through her like a fire igniting in dry straw. 'Whatever it takes, I'll do it!'

Nineve took her hands. 'You mean it, Guinevere? You'll really help?'

Gwen lifted her chin and met the Lady of the Lake's gaze. 'Yes,' she declared bravely. 'I will!'

As she spoke, the temperature of the air suddenly seemed to drop and there was a faint, sinister rumble of thunder in the sky above. Alarm flickered over Nineve's face as she glanced back towards the Lake. 'It's Morgana!' she whispered. 'While I am out of the water, my spell weakens. She must have sensed its strength fading.'

'What does that mean?' demanded Gwen.

'If Morgana feels the spell weakening, she will try and break through the magic barrier my spell holds in place.' A cold wind started to swirl around them, catching at their clothes. There was another rumble of thunder.

'She is coming!' Nineve cried.

4

A Magical Mission

'Wait here!' Nineve told the girls. 'It will be safer for you.' Turning round, she ran back into the Lake.

'Nineve!' Gwen cried, starting after her, but Flora grabbed her arm.

'She told us to wait here, Gwen!'

'But she might need our help!' Gwen struggled against her cousin's grip, but just then there was a flash of searing white lightning that made them both gasp. Flora clutched Gwen in fear.

Nineve reached the water and

stepped off the rock on to the surface of the Lake. She halted and held up one hand. 'Stop, Morgana! You may not cross my Lake!'

A freezing wind tossed the girls' hair around their faces and blew through the almost bare branches of the nearby apple tree. 'I'm scared!' Flora cried. Gwen felt torn, wanting to stay and comfort her cousin but also longing to go after Nineve and help her if she possibly could.

Thunder clapped overhead, making both girls jump. As the crashing sound faded it was replaced by a low chilling laugh that seemed to come from the very wind itself. Then, to their shock, they saw a woman's face begin to form in the whirling mist.

'Your spell is fading!' the woman hissed, her words whipping around them on the wind.

47

'It will still hold you, Morgana,' Nineve cried. 'You will not reach Avalon today.'

'The lunar eclipse approaches. And then the island will be mine. Give up now,' hissed Morgana.

'No!' gasped Gwen from the hillside.

'Shh!' Flora hushed her desperately.

'I will never give up. I will defend this island for as long as I can!' Nineve said. 'I command you to leave, Morgana.'

'No!'

'Yes! I command it.'

'You will fail, Nineve,' the wind-whipped voice shrieked, swirling the air around the island into a tempest. The wind howled, raging furiously and knocking both girls to the ground. Thunder crashed so violently it seemed to rip the skies apart . . . but then, suddenly, there was silence and stillness.

Gwen scrambled to her feet. 'Nineve?' she shouted anxiously.

'I am still here,' Nineve called to the girls. 'But I dare not leave the water again. Come—Morgana is frustrated

48

and angry but she has gone for now, and you may cross the Lake safely. It is time for you both to leave Avalon.'

Flora ran down the slope towards her.

Gwen took one last look around at the island. As she did so, the branches of the apple tree moved. Gwen frowned. There was no wind now, not even a slight breeze. But the branches were definitely stirring. They trembled and shook. Suddenly, the red apple fell to the floor and rolled straight to Gwen's feet. Gwen stared at it.

'Avalon has chosen to give you a gift, Guinevere!' Nineve called. 'Take it.'

Gwen picked the apple up and ran towards the Lake. She cradled the fruit in her hands, stroking its smooth red skin.

'That is no ordinary apple,' Nineve told her as she reached the shore. 'It's magical.'

Excitement leaped through Gwen. *More magic!* She held the apple as carefully as if it was made of glass. 'What can it do?'

'There is no single answer to that,' Nineve told her. 'All I can tell you is that its magic will be of use when you need it most. Keep it safe.'

Gwen slipped the apple into the bag around her waist and then she and Flora stepped on to the surface of the Lake and followed Nineve back through the mist. Gwen's mind was spinning with everything she had heard and seen since she had pulled the pendant from the rock. She barely noticed their journey across the water and back to the forest's edge.

'What do I have to do to free the sisters?' Gwen asked finally, as she and Flora stepped on to the rocks on the other side of the Lake.

'What do we have to do, you mean,' Flora corrected her.

Gwen looked at her cousin in

surprise. 'But Flora, you know you don't like adventures. I don't want to get you in any trouble,' she said, putting a hand on Flora's arm reassuringly. 'It's all right, really it is.'

'No! I can't let you go on your own. It would be much too dangerous. If you're going, I'm coming with you and that's that!' Flora's eyes, often so gentle, were fired with determination.

The Lady of the Lake nodded. 'Go together. You will help each other along the way.'

Gwen flashed a very grateful smile at Flora. She would have gone to free the sisters on her own without hesitating, but she couldn't help feeling glad that Flora was going to be coming with her. 'What do we have to do first?'

'I have been searching for the Spell Sisters using my magic,' Nineve explained, 'and I have discovered where Sophia, the sister who controls fire, is imprisoned.'

'Fire!' Flora breathed, her eyes wide.

'Where is she?' Gwen asked.

'My magic cannot tell you exactly where to go or how a sister is trapped, but it can give you clues. Watch carefully.' Nineve held up her closed fist and whispered a few words. Gwen couldn't understand the language, but the sound made her think of dry logs crackling in the grate at the castle.

Nineve opened her fingers and Gwen and Flora gasped as they saw a tiny burning flame resting on her palm. Nineve bent down and placed it on the water. It flared up and then, as it died down and disappeared, a picture appeared in the water. It showed a hill covered by thick brown ferns at the bottom and topped by a cluster of tall silver birch trees, their trunks pale and ghostly and their leaves autumn-gold.

'I believe Sophia is somewhere in this place,' Nineve said. 'I wish I could tell you more, but this is all my magic tells me. I am afraid you must try and find those things out for yourselves.'

'Oh!' Flora said suddenly. She had been staring at the picture and frowning. 'I think I can help, I'm sure I've seen that hill before!'

'Flora, that's wonderful!' said Gwen, smiling. She knew her cousin had a good memory for places. 'Where do you think it is?'

Flora studied the image. 'I was with Mother,' she said half to herself. 'I know we were travelling somewhere . . . yes, that's it!' She looked up, her eyes shining. 'It's a place called Silver Hill. It's near to Halston Castle, my aunt lives there.'

'We'll go there then, straight away!' said Gwen.

'May the luck of Avalon go with you,' said Nineve. 'Look carefully when you arrive there. Morgana's magic is strong, and Sophia may be disguised or transformed. You must remember that she could be anywhere or be anything.'

Gwen nodded seriously as Nineve continued.

'Now, listen carefully. To break the spell, you must use the pendant. Hold it against the place Sophia is trapped and say these words:

'Spell Sister of Avalon I now release;
Return to the island and help bring
peace.'

53

Gwen's hand went to the pendant around her neck and she repeated the spell in her head.

'Be brave and true, and listen to the words your heart speaks.' Nineve began to sink down into the Lake. 'Your quest is beginning, Guinevere. Remember, the fate of the kingdom is in your hands.'

'I won't forget,' Gwen vowed. 'And I won't fail you!'

Nineve vanished into the water. There was a faint ripple where she had been standing and then the surface was still.

Gwen and Flora stared at the water for a moment, but then the desire for action suddenly surged through Gwen. 'How do we get to Silver Hill, Flora?'

Flora looked worried. 'I think I can manage to find the way, but it will be at least half a day's travel. If we try and walk there, we won't be back until after suppertime. We'll be back so late that we'll get into dreadful trouble. Maybe we should wait until tomorrow?'

Gwen looked at her cousin in dismay. 'But if we wait until tomorrow we'll be wasting time. Can't we go now, please?'

Flora hesitated.

'Think of Avalon dying,' begged Gwen. 'We can't let that happen.'

Flora nodded firmly. 'You're right. We have to go now. This is far more important than us getting into trouble.'

Relief rushed through Gwen. She grabbed hold of her cousin's hand with a grin. 'What are we waiting for? Let's go!'

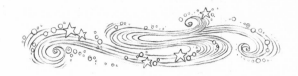

Journey by Moonlight!

Gwen and Flora set off eagerly through the forest. However, an hour later both of them were feeling hot and tired. Gwen's long hair clung damply to her neck and she was covered with scratches from the brambles and stray branches that reached across the paths.

'This is taking ages!' Flora exclaimed, pushing her long plaits back over her shoulders.

'We must be nearly at the other side of the forest now, though,' Gwen replied. 'You said we need to go through to the other side, right?'

'Yes, but then it's even further after that,' Flora said. 'At this rate, we're not going to get to Silver Hill until sunset. And what if— Whoops!'

Flora was interrupted as a branch she was trying to delicately push aside suddenly flicked back at her. Gwen smiled, and stopped to help her friend through the cluster of brambles. The sun was high in the sky. The long journey to Silver Hill was one problem, but when they got there, they had to find Sophia and try to free her. What if Morgana turned up again, and tried to stop them? Gwen swallowed, trying not to get too worried.

'I know it's far, Flora,' she said, 'but we don't have a choice. We have to rescue Sophia!'

Flora nodded, and linked arms with her cousin.

'You're right. Sorry, Gwen, I'm just a bit worried . . . and hungry!' Flora said.

Gwen dug in her bag. As well as the magic apple she had two pears from the castle orchard, along with a generous handful of raisins wrapped in a piece of cloth. She liked to keep some provisions in her bag, just in case she managed to escape from the castle into the forest. The pears were slightly bruised and the raisins dry and a bit tasteless, but they were better than nothing.

They walked on munching on their pears—even eating the core as they were so hungry. 'What's that?' Flora said suddenly.

'What?' Gwen asked, puzzled.

'Didn't you see it? There was something ahead of us, something white.' Flora quickly pointed. 'Look! There it is again!'

Gwen saw a pale shape flicking through the trees in front of them. It was an animal, a large one. She caught sight of ears, a tail, a sweeping mane . . .

'It's a horse!' she exclaimed. As she spoke, the animal disappeared into the shadows.

Gwen and Flora ran down the path until it opened out into a mossy clearing. On the other side of the glade was a beautiful horse with a long mane and tail and a coat as white as freshly fallen snow. As they came through the trees, he lifted his head and pricked his ears.

'What's he doing out here on his own?' breathed Flora.

'He hasn't got a saddle or bridle on,' said Gwen. 'He must be wild.'

The horse looked straight at her. Gwen felt strangely drawn to him, like a magnet to iron. She left Flora and started walking across the clearing.

'Gwen, what are you doing?' Flora called in alarm. 'If he's wild he might bite you . . . or kick you!'

'He won't.' Gwen held out her hand. 'Here, boy,' she murmured. The horse tossed his head and stared at her. Mischief lit up his eyes. Suddenly he whinnied, and then galloped straight towards her at top speed!

Flora squealed. For a moment all Gwen could think about was the horse bearing down on her, his eyes dark and flashing, his mane flying in a swirl of white. The ground shook under Gwen's feet as his hooves pounded into the short grass but, for some reason, she didn't feel scared. At the very last moment, the horse swerved and circled around her.

The wind lifted her hair as he passed. Trotting back to the far side of the clearing, the horse wheeled back, reared up and then plunged straight towards her again.

He just wants to play, Gwen realised as he dodged around her again. This time she whooped and chased him.

'Gwen, what are you doing?' Flora cried.

'Having fun!' Gwen laughed in delight, as she chased the wild horse. He broke into a canter and circled round and round her when she came to a stop in the middle of the clearing, her eyes on his. He was stunningly beautiful, his coat not having a single dapple or speck of grey.

At last the playfulness left the horse's eyes and he lowered his head and slowed to a trot, turning his ears towards her and reaching his neck down. Gwen had spent enough time with the castle horses to know this meant he was trying to say he wanted to be friends. She stepped away from him and turned slightly, lowering her eyes. She heard him stop and knew the horse was looking at her, then she felt the gentle thud of his hooves on the grass as he walked over to her. The horse stopped beside Gwen and lifted his head to her shoulder. She felt his warm breath tickling her neck and then quietly, so as not to scare him off, she turned and caressed him, feeling his silky mane running through her fingers. The horse pushed his head against her chest.

'Hey, boy,' she said softly, stroking his ears. 'Shall we be friends?'

The horse lifted his face to hers and breathed in and out. Gwen turned and walked towards Flora. The horse followed her.

Flora gaped in amazement. 'You've tamed him! I thought he was going to attack you at first.'

'He was just trying to play,' Gwen said, rubbing the horse's neck. 'He wanted to have some fun.'

Flora shook her head. 'You're so brave, Gwen. I'd have been terrified.'

'How could you be scared of a beautiful horse like this?' said Gwen, and the horse snorted as if in agreement.

'He is gorgeous,' Flora agreed. 'His coat is as pale as the moon.'

'That's perfect!' Gwen exclaimed. 'That's what I'll call him—Moonlight!'

A puzzled look crossed Flora's face. 'But why do you need to give him a name?'

'Well,' Gwen said slowly. 'We were just wondering how we could get to Silver Hill more quickly . . .'

Flora's eyes widened as she realised what Gwen meant. She started to shake her head vigorously. 'Oh no, Gwen! He hasn't got a saddle or a bridle, and anyway, if he's wild he'll never have been ridden before by anyone. No, Gwen! I'm not going to try and ride him. I'm not!'

Gwen's mind whirred. If they could ride on Moonlight they would get to Silver Hill much faster, but Flora was right. Gwen had often watched the stable-keeper at the castle breaking in horses, teaching them how to carry a rider, and she knew it took days—weeks even. How could they just get on a wild horse and ride him? She patted Moonlight thoughtfully, and as she did so her arm bumped against the bag around her waist.

The apple . . .

Gwen heard Nineve's voice echo through her head: *its magic will be of use when you need it most.*

Could the apple help?

Quickly, Gwen pulled it out. Her heart pounded as the horse caught the scent and pricked his ears. What if she was wrong and he just ate the apple and then it was gone, the magic all wasted? She held it out with a trembling hand.

'What are you doing?' whispered Flora.

Gwen swallowed. *Listen to the words your heart speaks,* Nineve had also said that to her. Every cell in her body was telling her this was the right thing to do. But what would happen?

Moonlight's teeth crunched into the apple. As he did so, an almost unbearably sweet fragrance spiralled into the air. Gwen was reminded of all of her favourite fruit in the world: ripe apricots, juicy plums, plump raspberries . . . She breathed in the scent in great gulps, but then something else happened that distracted her. Moonlight's white coat started to glow! 'Look!' she gasped, as the horse's mane began to sparkle as though every strand was coated in pearl dust.

'It's magic!' breathed Flora.

Gwen stared at the horse and then stroked his sparkling neck. 'Will you take us to Silver Hill?'

Moonlight snorted softly. If she'd imagined he'd understood her before, Gwen was now certain that he knew exactly what she meant.

She hesitated and then, taking him by his mane, led him to a nearby fallen tree. She climbed up onto the mossy trunk. Would the apple's magic really make him safe to ride? There was only one way to find out!

Putting her hands on his warm back, Gwen mounted the horse, hitching up her long skirts. Moonlight turned his head and sniffed at her right foot and then her left as if saying 'this is strange' but he stood as quietly as any of the riding horses in her uncle's stables.

'Come on!' Gwen urged Flora, excitement beating through her.

Flora still hesitated.

'Look—it's fine!' Gwen told her. 'He likes us—don't you, boy?' She patted Moonlight's neck encouragingly.

Flora sighed and ran over to the log. Taking Gwen's outstretched hand, she scrambled up to sit behind her on Moonlight's back. 'Oh goodness,' she said. 'This feels very peculiar. I've always wondered what it's like to ride bareback!'

'Just hold on tight to me!' Gwen wrapped her hands in Moonlight's mane and clicked her tongue. Flora grabbed Gwen's waist just in time as the horse lunged forward. To Gwen's surprise, she didn't feel in danger of falling off. Moonlight's movements were very smooth and riding him felt very different from short-legged, barrel-tummied Basil from the castle stables.

'But Gwen, how will we steer him to where we need to go?' exclaimed Flora as Moonlight headed through the trees at a canter.

'I think we can just . . . tell him!' Gwen said as she touched her heels to the horse's sides. 'Go on, boy! To the edge of the forest.'

At Gwen's contact Moonlight moved from a canter to the fastest gallop imaginable. The trees whipped by around them. Exhilaration rushed through Gwen as the world raced by. This was like flying! They burst out of the forest into a sunlit field.

'Oh my gosh! Oh my gosh!' Flora gasped over and over again, hanging on to Gwen with a tight grip.

Gwen yelled in excitement. 'Faster, Moonlight! Faster!' The wind whipped away her words, tossing them high into the cornflower-blue sky as Moonlight galloped like the north wind across the grass!

A Steep Climb

Moonlight raced through meadows, along tracks and through shady tunnels of trees. As they sped through the countryside Gwen and Flora caught glimpses of big, slow carts being pulled along; people working near small crofts and cottages; sheep grazing in fields and children fishing in small streams.

'Th-that's it! Keep going—past that fallen oak and then over the bridge!' Flora shouted, clinging on to Gwen for dear life. The horse seemed to

69

understand the directions, and nobody seemed to notice them as they raced by. Moonlight's pace didn't falter as his hooves ate up the miles. Gwen clung on to his mane feeling like she was on a fairy horse from one of the old tales the storytellers wove as they sat in the great hall beside the fire. She had never imagined it was possible to go so fast! If she hadn't been so keen to rescue Sophia, Gwen would have wished the ride could go on forever.

'There it is. There's Silver Hill!' cried Flora at last.

Gwen saw a steep hill up ahead with a grove of silver birch trees covering its top. It looked just like the picture that Nineve had conjured on the surface of the Lake.

Moonlight galloped straight towards the hill and, for a moment, Gwen thought they were going to crash into its steep sides! However, as the ground started to rise, the horse slowed to a trot and then came to a halt near a stream that flowed down from the mountain. Moonlight was breathing hard from the exercise, but his eyes were bright and clear.

Gwen hugged his neck. 'You got us here. Thank you, Moonlight!'

He snorted happily. Gwen dismounted, and then helped Flora off the horse's back too. Rubbing Moonlight's nose, Gwen looked up at the hill and frowned. The sides were steep at the base, even steeper further up, and the hill was covered with thick golden-coloured ferns with no obvious path through them. 'You'd better stay here,' she told Moonlight reluctantly.

Flora nodded. 'It's too difficult for him to climb and there's water and grass for him down here. He'll be fine. But what can we tie him up with?'

'I don't think he needs tying up,' Gwen said looking at the horse. 'You'll wait for us, won't you, boy?'

Moonlight gave her a gentle push with his nose. Gwen was sure it was his way of saying yes. 'We'll be back soon,' she promised, hugging his neck.

'And thank you for the ride,' Flora told him, patting his side.

Gwen adjusted the bow and arrows on her back and then the two girls

71

set off up the hill. The dry ferns were hard to walk through, catching at their ankles and knees as if they were trying to slow them down, but Gwen and Flora marched on undaunted.

'I wonder what Sophia will be like?' Gwen said.

'And how we'll find her,' put in Flora. 'Where do you think Morgana will have imprisoned her?'

'Hopefully it will be obvious when we get there,' Gwen replied.

If we get there, she thought, worry flicking through her like a flame as she looked at the climb ahead. The ferns were thinning now, replaced by tufts of grass and treacherous patches of loose stones and slippery moss which were difficult to walk on. The slope seemed to be getting a lot steeper too.

Gwen stopped as the land rose up in a steep incline that was almost like a cliff face. 'We're going to have to climb this bit,' she said, turning to Flora. She grabbed some of the long grass as a handhold and started pulling herself up the slope. Gwen was used to climbing—she often climbed trees and rocks in the forest near the castle—but she'd only gone a few metres when she heard Flora's voice below. 'Gwen, I can't do it!'

Gwen glanced down. Flora was looking up at her helplessly. 'I can't climb all the way up there!'

Gwen hesitated and then slithered back down the slope. She tore her dress on a spur of rock, but she didn't care. 'Come on, Flora. You can do it!' she encouraged her cousin.

Flora chewed her lip and shook her head. 'I can't. I really can't.'

Gwen wondered what to do. She knew Flora really wasn't used to climbing. 'All right. Don't worry. You stay here and rest. I'll go up to the top by myself.'

'No!' Flora exclaimed. 'Nineve said we should work together. You might need me and we have to rescue Sophia as quickly as we can.'

Gwen nodded, looking up at the slope again. 'Well, maybe I can help you. If you go in front of me, I'll tell you where to look for handholds. You just need to use the grass and bits of rock to pull yourself up.'

Flora swallowed.

'I know you can do it, Flora! And I'll be with you the whole way.'

'All right. I'll try,' Flora said resolutely.

Gwen showed her where the first few handholds were and Flora started to edge her way up the cliff face. 'That's it!' Gwen encouraged. She waited at the bottom. It was better to give advice staying where she was, standing back and looking up at her cousin. 'Go to your right a bit. It's easier that way . . .'

Gradually, Flora began to get more confident and went a bit faster, starting to find the handholds and footholds on her own. Gwen breathed a sigh of relief and moved towards the slope, but just as she was about to start climbing herself, she heard Flora cry out.

Gwen's gaze shot upwards. The clump of grass Flora had been holding on to had pulled away from the hillside, sending Flora tumbling downwards, her hands and feet sending stones flying.

'Gwen! Help!' Flora screamed . . .

7

Trapped!

Gwen watched in horror as Flora fell towards her. Just as she was sure her cousin was going to slide down the entire slope, Flora somehow managed to grab a tree stump, stopping her fall. She clung to the hillside, her face pale, her legs swinging.

'Gwen!' she gasped.

'You're all right,' Gwen called. Her own heart was pounding but she tried to stay calm for Flora's sake. Panicking would be the worst thing either of them could do. Flora was still about halfway up and if she fell now, she might land on hard rock and really hurt herself. 'Wait, I'll come up and help you,' she said quickly.

'No, I can do it.' Flora frowned in determination and reached out to start climbing again. She found a tree root to hold on to and put her weight on it.

'Be careful!' Gwen cried as she saw the tree root move. 'That doesn't look very safe . . .'

Her words were drowned out by Flora's squeal as the root started to come away from the hillside!

'Hold on!' Gwen cried. She frantically tried to think of a way to save Flora. Suddenly she whipped an arrow from her quiver and slipped the bow off her shoulder. Maybe she could shoot through Flora's cloak and stop her falling that way? No, that would be far too risky. Then an idea came to her. She couldn't shoot at Flora but . . . Gwen notched the arrow to the string and in a single, smooth movement, heaved the string back with her right hand. Breathing out,

Gwen released the arrow, and followed it with another, then another. The three arrows flew swiftly from her bow and hit the slope, striking into the soil, their shafts quivering. 'Grab hold of the arrows!' Gwen yelled to Flora as the tree root finally gave way.

Flora reached out desperately as she slid past Gwen's arrows. The first arrow gave way, but the second and third held firm. Flora swung from them, her legs kicking.

'Keep still!' Gwen called out. She could see the danger wasn't over yet. The arrows could snap or come loose at any moment. Gwen threw down her bow and quiver and started to climb the slope. She had to get to her cousin and help her. 'Don't move, Flora! You're making it worse!'

But even as she spoke, the two arrows both snapped at the same time and Flora shrieked as she crashed down the slope into Gwen. The two girls tumbled down the steep hill, rolling over and over until they came to a stop in the thick bracken below.

For a moment, Gwen just lay there in the grass, blinking up at the blue sky. She tried to move her arms and legs. She was a bit bruised, but nothing seemed to be broken. 'Flora?' she called anxiously, sitting up.

Her cousin was a few metres away, also just beginning to sit up. There were brown fronds caught in her neat plaits, soil smudges on her cheeks and her cloak was torn.

'Are you all right?' Gwen asked.

'Y–yes.' Flora blinked.

Gwen felt a rush of relief. And then she started to giggle. Flora looked as startled as a fawn and completely unlike her usual lady-like self.

'What are you laughing at?' Flora demanded.

'You look really funny!' Gwen started to laugh harder.

Indignation flashed through Flora's eyes. 'Well, how am I expected to look? I've just fallen down the hillside that you made me climb, and you've been shooting arrows at me!'

For a moment Gwen thought her cousin was really cross with her, but then she saw the teasing glint in Flora's blue eyes as she began to smile.

'You could at least have caught me! Oh, and by the way, you should see yourself. You've got a worm on your head!' Flora said with amusement. Gwen reached up, and her hand landed straight on a squishy worm. 'Yuck!' she

cried, pulling it out of her red hair.

Flora burst into a torrent of giggles at Gwen's expression. Gwen saw the funny side and the next minute the two of them had collapsed back into the bracken, laughing together.

But their laughter soon faded as they remembered the task at hand. Getting their breath back, Gwen and Flora got to their feet.

'Oh, Gwen, what are we going to do? We've still got to get to the top of the hill,' Flora pointed out. 'Poor Sophia's trapped somewhere up there and we have to free her as soon as possible.'

'Let's look for a different way up,' Gwen replied.

They collected Gwen's bow and quiver and quickly walked round the hillside until they found a gentler slope to climb. With Gwen's help, and Flora being extra careful about what she used for a handhold, they finally managed to get to the very top. The crown of the hill was gently rounded, covered with short grass and a mass of silver birch trees that surrounded a small clearing.

'Oh goodness, aren't the trees

beautiful?' Flora breathed as she walked between the slender trunks.

Gwen nodded. The birches had silvery white bark and the leaves overhead were yellow and bronze. The air amongst the trees was strangely still, almost as though it was waiting for something to happen. Gwen was reminded of the Lake. There was the same feeling of magic here in the birch glade.

But the beauty and feeling of magic couldn't distract her from what they had come there to do. 'We've got to find Sophia!' she said, looking round anxiously. 'But where could she be?'

'There's nothing that looks like a prison here,' said Flora.

'What about those rocks?' Gwen pointed to a cluster of grey boulders in the clearing.

The girls went over to them. The rocks were tall, bigger than them. But there was no sign of anyone trapped there.

Gwen began to feel panicky. 'There isn't anything here, just trees and rocks. Maybe Sophia isn't imprisoned here after all. Morgana could have moved her somewhere else!'

'Wait!' Flora said suddenly. 'Don't you remember what the Lady of the Lake said? She told us to look carefully because Sophia could be anywhere or be anything. So, maybe. . . ' She gazed round the clearing, her eyes widening. 'Sophia is trapped inside one of these rocks or in one of the trees?'

Gwen could have hugged her. 'Oh, Flora! Of course! After all, it was the trees that Nineve's magic flame on the Lake showed us, wasn't it?' She glanced round at the silver birches and her face fell. 'But how will we know which one? There are so many of them.'

Flora ran over and started examining the nearest tree trunk. 'Maybe there's a clue somewhere.'

Gwen had another idea. 'What about the pendant? It might be able to help.' Taking hold of it, she held it up. The glowing blue gem caught the rays of the afternoon sun. It glittered and shone, sparkling like a river in sunshine. Gwen watched it, waiting for a sign, something—anything—that would help her discover where Sophia was. 'Come on,' she muttered to it. 'Help us! Please!'

But the pendant just winked at her in the sun. Gwen sighed in frustration and put it back around her neck. It looked like they really were going to have to check every tree one by one. It was going to take hours!

'Gwen!' She heard Flora's intake of breath.

'What?' Gwen swung round.

'Come here! Look at this tree . . . it's different!' Flora was standing by one of the smallest, most slender birch trees near the edge of the clearing. She beckoned Gwen over.

'It looks just the same as all the others to me,' said Gwen as she walked over to where Flora was standing.

'No. Look properly.' Flora pointed to the trunk and then Gwen saw what Flora's sharp eyes had already spotted. The trunk was a slightly different colour from the other trees. Instead of being a pale ghostly white, it had a definite coppery tinge, and its leaves glinted red in the sunlight—like fire!

'Maybe this is where Sophia is trapped!' Flora said excitedly.

Gwen's heart skipped a beat. Could Flora be right? Now she was looking more closely too, she could see that there were other differences from the rest of trees. This one had smoother bark and not a single leaf had fallen from its branches. 'But how do we find out for sure?'

Flora looked at her. 'I don't know.'

Gwen cautiously touched the bark of the tree. 'Hello?' Immediately, her fingers started to tingle. It was the same feeling she'd

85

had when she'd first pulled the pendant from the rock. 'Sophia? Are you in there? The Lady of the Lake sent us. I'm Gwen and this is my cousin, Flora.'

As Gwen spoke, the tree seemed to shiver and an image started to form in the bark. The girls gasped. It was the face of a beautiful young woman! Gwen realised that Sophia wasn't just trapped inside the tree—she *was* the tree. Her sad eyes were pleading, and to Gwen and Flora's surprise, her mouth moved.

'Help me!' The words seemed to whisper in the air like the sound of leaves rustling in a breeze. 'Set me free!'

'We will! Don't worry!' Gwen promised. 'Oh, I'm so glad we've found you!'

Keeping one hand on the bark, she

fumbled for the pendant with the other hand. The spell. She just had to say the spell!

But as Gwen reached for the blue gem, she heard a hideous cawing sound, like jackdaws screaming—only ten times as loud. Flora looked over her shoulder and cried out in alarm. Gwen heard the panic in her cousin's voice and looked round too. What she saw filled her with an icy horror.

A flock of evil-looking birds was swooping across the sky towards the hilltop. Their bodies were black as coal and their red beaks sharp and pointed. They had huge wings that were as large as an eagle's and, worst of all, their tails crackled with magical bolts of lightning.

Flora gave a choking cry. 'Th-they're going to attack us!'

'Morgana must have sent them!' cried Gwen as the birds darted towards them, their sparking tails lighting up the sky. 'She wants to stop us freeing Sophia!'

Flora looked at Gwen in terror. 'What are we going to do?'

8

A Daring Rescue

Gwen felt fear rise inside her as she saw the flock of enormous magic birds flying towards them, curved talons reaching out and beaks opening wide. But this was no time to be scared. She pulled an arrow out of her quiver and eased the bow from her shoulder. She didn't even have to think about what to do; the arrow was instantly notched, the string pulled back against her cheek. The lightning-tailed birds shrieked as they closed in.

Gwen couldn't bring herself to actually hurt the birds, but she had to scare them away. She aimed at the leading bird. She knew from all her practice that she had to aim in front of the bird, to allow for its swift movement through the air. She let her arrow fly and it whizzed right in front of the bird, just missing its beak—but for once, Gwen wasn't trying to hit her target. With a squawk, the bird swerved in the sky with a shower of sparks and frantically flapping wings, then flew away from them. But Gwen didn't watch it go—she was already lifting another arrow. Aim. . . Release!

Her arrows flew through the air, one after the other, so quickly that the lightning-tailed birds were swerving left and right. They squawked angrily, swooping away from the barrage of Gwen's arrows.

'You're doing it, Gwen!' Flora cried. 'Keep going!'

But even though she was shooting as quickly as she could, Gwen couldn't release the arrows fast enough to scare off all the birds. They swooped down through the sky, the sparks from their flashing tails raining down towards the ground and setting the top branches of the trees alight.

Gwen suddenly had a new worry— if one of the sparks landed on her or Flora, their cloaks would go up in flames!

'Quick!' she gasped, grabbing Flora. She pulled her over to the nearby boulders, a shower of sparks falling exactly where they had just been standing.

Flora grabbed some of the smaller rocks from the ground and threw them as hard as she could, trying to help Gwen scare the birds off. 'Just keep going!' panted Gwen. 'We can do it!' But despite her brave words, she knew they were in desperate trouble. There were too many birds, and Sophia was still trapped inside the tree. She reached into her quiver. She only had one more arrow left!

What are we going to do? The question bounced through her head.

Flora screamed as a large burning branch broke off from the canopy above and crashed near to them on the grass. Flames licked the ground and sparks jumped onto the surrounding trees, smoke swirling in grey plumes amongst the tree trunks. Suddenly, in a burst, the tree next to Sophia's caught fire!

'Sophia!' cried Gwen in horror. Forgetting all thoughts of her own safety, she jumped out from behind the boulders. The birds flew at her, pecking and clawing, their talons and beaks raking at her hair and eyes, but Gwen fought her way through them, swinging her bow like a weapon. What if Sophia

was burned alive in her tree-prison? She couldn't bear it.

Behind her, Gwen could hear Flora yelling at her to come back but she ignored her. She had to reach the tree and help Sophia!

Thankfully the birds didn't seem to like the smoke at all and as it grew thicker, they retreated upwards into the branches. They perched there, shrieking furiously.

Gwen blocked them out of her mind as she entered the dark cloud of smoke around the trees. Her eyes stung and her lungs filled with smoke, making

her cough. Pulling her cloak over her face, she fought her way to Sophia's tree. She could feel the heat from the burning birch next to it, but to her utter relief she saw that it hadn't actually caught fire yet.

Throat burning and eyes watering, Gwen pulled the blue pendant over her head and held it desperately against the bark. She chanted the magic spell:

'Spell Sister of Avalon, I now release;
Return to the island, and help
bring peace!'

As she gasped out the last word, the tree shimmered all over and then started to tremble and shake. Gwen staggered back with a cry. What was going on?

Around her the smoke thickened and the flames leaped higher, but Gwen didn't notice. Her eyes were fixed on the enchanted tree. As she gazed at it, the tree started to shrink and change shape! Its slender silver trunk became a female body dressed in a silver gown, and its branches and copper leaves became a cascade of vivid red hair. The next instant, the entire tree had disappeared! Instead, a beautiful young woman stood in its place, her hair held back from her face by silver and green ribbons.

'Sophia!' whispered Gwen.

The older girl started to smile and nod but then suddenly exclaimed in alarm. 'Watch out, Guinevere!'

Gwen heard the falling branch at exactly the same moment. Some instinct deep within her made her leap to one side. The bough crashed down beside her, sending sparks flying into the air. One fell on Gwen's cloak, and the material caught fire! Gwen's heart skipped a beat as she saw the flames leap up.

But then, above everything—over

the sound of the screeching and cawing of the birds, Flora's screaming and the crackling of the flames—came the sound of a calm, musical voice:

'Burning fire, shooting flame
Mine to order, mine to tame.'

Gwen realised it was Sophia chanting. She wasn't shouting but somehow her voice rang out loud and clear, with a deep ancient magic that cut through all the noise and flames. Despite her panic at her cloak being on fire, Gwen stared at the sorceress in awe. Her eyes were burning, her face pale, and the air around her seemed to crackle with magical energy.

'Cease, flames!' Sophia called, opening her arms wide. 'Sophia commands you!'

Every flame Gwen could see suddenly seemed to freeze mid-flicker and then, in the blink of an eye, they winked out and were gone!

For a long moment, nothing moved in the cloud of thick grey smoke that rose from the charred branches and

Gwen's cloak.

'You . . . you saved me,' Gwen stammered. From outside the cloud of smoke she could still hear the birds shrieking and Flora desperately calling her name, but somehow inside the cloud of smoke it was like a separate peaceful little world.

A smile crossed Sophia's beautiful face. 'Yes. And you rescued me, despite great danger to yourself.'

Gwen coughed and rubbed her eyes, then returned Sophia's smile. 'Well, I couldn't just let you burn!' she said. 'We need you—and all the sisters of Avalon, if we're going to stop Morgana!'

A moment later, the smoke started to thin and fade. Flora saw Gwen and yelled in relief, jumping out from behind the rocks. But as she did so, Gwen realised that now the smoke was clearing, she could see the lightning-tailed birds were still waiting high up in the trees. They caught sight of the girls, and with a

fierce screech, the
flock rose from
their perch in
the branches and
swooped down,
aiming straight for
Gwen and Flora
with their sharp beaks.

'Enough!' Sophia's voice snapped out. She thrust her hands into the air. Two balls of orange fire burst from her fingertips as she opened her palms. Glowing brightly, the two fireballs shot upwards into the flock.

The birds tried to stop, swerving away and flying back up towards the branches, but Sophia hurled two more fireballs at them. Screeching in unison, the birds turned tail and finally flew away from Silver Hill. Gwen and Flora sighed with relief.

'My sister Morgana's pets,' Sophia said, watching grimly as the birds became just a black blot against the sky and then disappeared.

'Oh, Gwen!' Flora reached her cousin and hugged her. 'I'm so glad you're OK. I didn't know what was

98

happening. I couldn't see anything through the smoke.'

'Sophia stopped the fire with her magic and saved me,' Gwen said, smiling at the sorceress.

Flora turned to the sorceress with awe. 'Thank you so much!'

'It is I who should be thanking both of you.' Sophia pirouetted, the hem of her silver dress sweeping around her in a wide circle and a look of joy on her face. 'I am free again! I thought I would be trapped forever.'

'Nineve sent us,' Gwen explained. 'Now we've released you, we're going to find your sisters and free them too.'

'Before Morgana has the power to take over Avalon forever,' Flora added.

'Morgana will never have Avalon!' Gwen declared. 'We'll stop her!'

Sophia looked from Gwen to Flora and smiled. 'Morgana certainly has more of a fight on her hands than she realises. I will hope with all my heart that you succeed.'

'But for now, it's time we returned to Avalon!' Gwen said. 'Shall we go?'

Sophia nodded. 'Of course.' She held out her hands to them both. 'To Avalon!'

9

Return to Avalon

Gwen and Flora scrambled down the hill together, holding on to roots and grass. Sophia moved swiftly and lightly beside them, her feet barely seeming to touch the ground. As they reached the bottom, they heard a loud whinny, and Moonlight came cantering out of a nearby group of trees.

Delight rushed through Gwen. 'Hello, boy.' Moonlight thrust his head against her and she stroked his face and ears. 'Did you miss us?'

He lifted his face to hers and breathed out in reply. She saw the happiness in his dark eyes that they were back with him again.

'How are we all going to get back home?' Flora said suddenly. 'Moonlight can't carry all three of us, and if we walk it will take ages.'

'Do not worry,' Sophia told her. 'I can use my magic to transport myself back to the Lake. I will be there before you and will tell Nineve how brave you both were.' She touched Moonlight's face, her eyes meeting his. 'Carry them safely back,' she whispered.

Gwen smiled. 'Not too safely, though —I want to go fast again!'

She leaped up onto Moonlight's back and helped Flora up behind her.

Sophia raised her hands and clapped them together. The next instant she had vanished.

Gwen touched her heels to Moonlight's sides, and with another joyful whinny he set off at a gallop.

It was just as exhilarating to race home on Moonlight's back—more so because Gwen had the happiness inside of knowing that the first task had been completed successfully. She and Flora had freed Sophia! As Moonlight raced across the meadows and fields, Gwen turned to her cousin. 'Thank you for coming with me up to the top of the hill, Flora. I'd never have found Sophia without you.'

'We'd never have got there if you hadn't thought about using Moonlight! And you were the brave one who went through the fire to save Sophia before it was too late. She would have burned if it hadn't been for you,' said Flora.

'We both helped in our own way,' Gwen said. She squeezed Flora's hand. 'I'm so glad we're going to be freeing all the sisters together.'

'I'm glad too,' said Flora. 'I'd never realised how much fun going on an adventure could be!'

They smiled happily at each other as Moonlight entered the forest near the Lake. He swerved through the trees and finally came to a halt by the glimmering water. Sophia was standing on the rocks talking to Nineve, who was in the Lake, the bottom of her long hair floating out behind her. They both waved to the girls as they arrived.

Gwen and Flora dismounted and joined them. 'You have done so well,' Nineve told them, her eyes sparkling. She opened her arms and they reached over to hug her. 'Sophia has been telling me everything that has happened. Come. Let us go over to the island now.'

The Lady of the Lake clapped her hands, and the same fine white mist as before swirled around Gwen and Flora and lifted them on to the water. This time, neither girl hesitated. They ran across the surface of the Lake beside Nineve and Sophia and into the purple mist that surrounded Avalon.

When they reached the shore, Sophia darted onto the rocks. Her face shone with relief. 'Avalon! It's so good to be back. I never thought I would see it again.'

'I just wish we'd freed all your sisters already and the island was as beautiful as it used to be,' said Gwen.

'I have hope that you will succeed. But for now, I can make Avalon more cheerful in my own way,' said Sophia. 'Come to the house with me!'

The girls looked at the Lady of the Lake, who smiled and nodded. 'Go. I will wait here in the water.'

The girls followed Sophia up the steps to the house, past the apple tree whose gift had been so important. The house was dusty inside, the floors bare and the cupboards empty. A lonely fire of kindling and logs was set unlit in the grate.

Sophia pointed at it. 'Fire. I command you!'

A blue spark flew from her fingers. It hit the wood and the kindling and the logs instantly burst into warm flames. The orange and gold light made the whole house seem somehow much brighter. Looking into the flames, Gwen felt a glow come over her. This was no ordinary fire—this was a *magical* fire. She knew it would keep the island warm until Sophia's sisters returned.

'I am finally home again,' Sophia said. 'And for that, I thank you both from the bottom of my heart.'

'We're just happy we could help,' said Gwen.

'I wish I could come with you on your adventures and help you free my seven sisters,' said Sophia. 'But I must remain here now to keep the magic of Avalon from dying further. However, I want to give you something that will help you on your travels.'

She pointed at the fire once more, and clicked her fingers. A burning red coal jumped out onto the stone hearth.

Sophia passed her fingers over it, whispering a word the girls could not understand. Before their eyes it turned from glowing red to a pale shining white stone which seemed to have flames of bronze and copper leaping through its centre.

'It is a fire agate gemstone,' Sophia said, picking it up and holding it out to Gwen. 'If you succeed in your quest to free my sisters, each of them will

also give you a gem. These gifts shall help give you the strength you need to defeat Morgana.'

'Thank you,' Gwen said, staring at the stone. Sophia held the beautiful gem out towards Gwen, and then there was a fiery flash. To both the girls' amazement, the gemstone floated through the air and attached itself to Gwen's necklace. One pale stone with a heart of fire now  rested next to the pendant that came from the depths of the Lake.

Gwen touched it and felt her fingertips tingle.

'You should go now,' Sophia said softly. 'Good luck with finding my sisters. May Avalon's magic go with you.'

'Thank you,' Gwen told her. 'We'll do everything we can.'

'Everything,' echoed Flora.

They embraced Sophia and then, leaving her beside the glowing fireplace, Gwen and Flora ran down the stone steps of the house, to the Lake where Nineve was waiting for them.

'Come,' she said, smiling, and led them back across the Lake.

When they reached the other side and stepped out onto the rock, Nineve started to drift down into the glassy, still water. 'Remember, girls—there are still seven Spell Sisters to find and free. I will use my magic to search for them. When I have found where another is trapped, I will contact you through the pendant.'

'We'll be waiting!' Gwen vowed.

With a smile, Nineve disappeared into the Lake.

Gwen and Flora looked at each other. 'Gosh! So much has happened today,' Gwen said.

Flora glanced up at the sun setting in the sky. 'And look how late it is! Everyone in the castle is bound to be wondering where we are.'

They climbed back onto Moonlight.

When they reached the edge of the forest, he stopped and the girls dismounted again. 'What are we going to do with him? We can't just take him back to the castle and say we found him,' Flora pointed out.

Gwen looked at the beautiful horse. Flora was right. Even if they could explain finding Moonlight, they would never be allowed to keep and ride a horse like him. Her uncle would take him as his own. 'What do you think, boy?' she asked.

Moonlight glanced round at the trees and then pawed at the ground. Gwen thought she understood. 'You think you should stay here?'

Moonlight snorted. There was grass to graze and water to drink. Gwen knew he would be fine. 'Stay here then. We'll come and find you again when Nineve summons us back to the Lake.'

She and Flora both hugged the pale, sparkling horse. He nuzzled them and they said goodbye. As they left the forest, Gwen turned to wave one last time, but Moonlight had already gone, melting like mist into the trees.

+ + +

'Flora! Guinevere! Where have you been?' As they neared the castle gates, Aunt Matilda came hurrying across the drawbridge and down the hill towards them, holding her long skirts up. 'Everyone's looking for you! We've been searching the barns, the vegetable gardens, the mill pond, the . . . oh!' She broke off with a shocked cry. 'Look at the state of the pair of you! Whatever has happened?'

Gwen looked down at her torn and stained clothes and then at Flora, who looked just as bad.

'We're sorry, Mother,' Flora said quickly. 'We . . . er . . . we . . .'

'We got lost,' said Gwen hastily. 'Collecting herbs, in the forest. We're really very sorry, Aunt Matilda. We've been wandering around for ages and ages.'

Her aunt looked at them. 'But where are your herb baskets?'

'We lost them on the way,' Gwen said quickly.

111

'We're really very sorry, Mother,' Flora added.

Lady Matilda looked at their smudged faces and suddenly gathered them into a hug. 'Oh, I'm just glad you're safe, my dears,' she said, pulling them in tight.

As they walked back through the courtyard, Gwen saw a group of the pages watching them and whispering to one another. She wasn't so interested in what they had been up to, now that she and Flora had been having so many adventures of their own!

'We really have been so very worried. It sounds like you've had a terrible time,' said Aunt Matilda.

Gwen bit back her grin. 'Oh, it wasn't that bad.'

'We must go in and call off the search,' declared her aunt. 'And you can both have some supper. Your adventures are over!'

'For today,' Gwen whispered to Flora as Aunt Matilda set off for the castle, her skirt sweeping around her like a ship in full sail.

Flora's blue eyes shone. 'But

soon they'll start all over again,' she whispered back.

Gwen laughed and grabbed her hand. Together they ran back into the castle while behind them the setting sun sank into the tall trees.

A magic fire burnt inside the massive hollowed out trunk of an oak tree. The flames did not leap up in a cheerful gold and orange, but flickered an ink black and deepest midnight blue, sucking the light from the wooden chamber.

Morgana Le Fay stood by the flames. Her long dark hair was caught back with a headband made of glittering polished beads of jet and golden thorns. Her black eyes glittered as the flames suddenly flickered and died, leaving just a smouldering log. In the centre of the smoke an image formed. It showed two girls standing on a hillside between silver birch trees, fighting off a flock of enormous black birds. Then it showed one of the trees changing and turning into a woman, and finally an image of her embracing the two girls.

'So, my lightning birds failed. Sophia has been freed,' Morgana snarled. She snapped her fingers over the fire, but only a few faint sparks leaped from her fingers. They fell to the half-burnt wood, but nothing happened. Morgana's eyes flashed with fury and she hissed a curse as she realised the truth. Now Sophia was free, the power Morgana had stolen from her sister had been returned. She was no longer able to control fire.

'Those girls have managed to thwart me this time,' Morgana muttered, 'but next time they try they will not succeed. If they try to rescue the other sisters of Avalon, I will stop them. Then they will be truly sorry . . .'

Morgana went over to the entrance of the hollowed out tree. For a moment she stood there silhouetted against the star-filled sky, and then she rubbed her hands together. 'Yes, they will be very sorry.'

Laughing evilly, she strode out into the shadows of the waiting trees.